FUNNY JOKES FOR

FOR

YEAR OLD KIDS

BY
JIMMY JONES

Hundreds of really funny, hilarious jokes that will have the kids in fits of laughter in no time!

They're all in here - the funniest
- Jokes
- Riddles
- Tongue Twisters
- Knock Knock Jokes

for 8 year old kids!

Funny kids love funny jokes and this brand new collection of original and classic jokes promises hours of fun for the whole family!

Books by Jimmy Jones

Funny Jokes For Funny Kids
Knock Knock Jokes For Funny Kids

Funny Jokes For Kids Series
All Ages 5 -12!

To see all the latest books by
Jimmy Jones just go to
kidsjokebooks.com

Contents

Funny Jokes!

What happened to the leopard who had 4 baths in one day?

He was spotless!

What did the skeleton order at the restaurant?

A glass of water and a mop!

Why did the egg hide?

It was a little chicken!

What did the hedgehog say to the cactus?
Hi dad!

Why was the mommy kangaroo sad when it rained?
The kids had to play inside!

What sort of music do frogs listen to?
Hip Hop!

What do you have if an elephant sits on your friend?
A flat mate!

Why did the chewing gum cross the road?
It was stuck to the chicken's foot!

What did the big cow say to the small cow?
Moooooove over!

Why did the boy laugh after his time in hospital?

The doctor had him in stitches!

Why was the boy so wet when he got to school?

He came in a car pool!

What game do astronauts play?

Moonopoly!

Where did the butcher go on Saturday night?

The Meatball!

What was the ghost's favorite ride at the playground?

The ScaryGoRound!

What does a witch do when her broom stops suddenly?

She flies off the handle!

Why do wasps get so much done in a day?
They are busy bees!

Why did the farmer put sugar on his crops?
So he could grow sweet potatoes!

What happened to the 2 rabbits when they fell in love?
They lived hoppily ever after!

Why did the golfer go to the dentist?
She had a hole in one!

What do you call a dinosaur with only one eye?
A Do-You-Think-They-Saurus!

What did the snake give his girlfriend after their first date?
A goodnight hiss!

What kind of books do skunks read?
Best Smellers!

Why was the spaceman acting so strange?
He was an Astro-nut!

What do you call a skeleton that sleeps in?
Lazy Bones!

Why did Humpty Dumpty love autumn so much?

He had a great fall!

What do you hear if you cross Bambi with a ghost?

Bamboooo!

What was the drummer's favorite vegetable?

Beets!

Why was the detective duck given the key to the city?

He quacked the case!

What do you call a cow in a washing machine?

A milkshake!

What did the teeth say to the gums?

The dentist is taking us out tonight!

Why do bananas put on so much sunscreen at the beach?

Otherwise they might peel!

If you lend money to a bison, what is it?

A Buff A Loan!

Why was the basketball court really slippery?

The players love to dribble!

Why did the raspberry call 911?
She was in a jam!

What do you call a pig with no personality?
A boar!

Why did the man have to leave the car assembly line?
He took too many brakes!

What do you hear after 2 porcupines have a kiss?

Ouch!

Why is a guitar opposite to a fish??

A guitar can be tuned but you can't tuna fish!

Why was it so hot at the basketball game?

Most of the fans had left!

Why is it no fun to play cards in Africa?
Too many cheetahs!

If you are really cold and grumpy what do you eat?
A brrrgrrr!

What would happen if you crossed a centipede with a parrot?
You get a walkie talkie!

Why is the ocean always so clean?
Mermaids!

What do you get if you cross an owl with a comet?
A hooting star!

What do you call vampire pigs?
Frankenswine!

How does a bee get to work?
He waits at the buzz stop!

What has a bottom at the top?
Your legs!

Why was the deer at the dentist?
He had buck teeth!

What did the frog have for lunch?
A diet croak with french flies!

What do puppies eat at the movies?
Pupcorn!

Where did the car go for a swim?
The carpool!

What would you call it if worms took over the entire world?

Global Worming!

Why did the snail avoid the drive through?

He didn't like fast food!

What do you get if you cross a ghost with a pair of trousers?

Scaredy Pants!

Why did the chicken cross the playground?
To get to the other slide!

How do planets stay clean?
They have a meteor shower!

Why was the astronaut so happy?
He was over the moon!

What do garbage trucks eat for lunch?
Junk Food!

What happens if you cross a computer and a life guard?
You get a screensaver!

Why did the frog say Mooooo?
He was learning another language!

What do you call a girl giving a boy a piggyback?

Carrie!

What do you call a boy giving a girl a piggyback?

Carter!

What kind of dog can tell the time?

A watch dog!

What is an astronaut's favorite snack?
A Mars Bar!

What should you eat if you have a cold?
Maccaroni and Sneeze!

Why was the computer feeling old?
It was losing it's memory!

Why do mice take really long showers?
They like to feel squeaky clean!

What did the vampire get when he bit the snowman?
Frostbite!

What do you use to wrap a cloud?
A rainbow!

Why were the ghosts hired as cheerleaders?
They had so much spirit!

Where did the really cool mouse live?
In his mousepad!

What can you use to open the great lakes?
The Florida Keys!

What do you call a pig that was caught speeding?

A road hog!

How did the fish know how much he weighed?

He used his scales!

Why do birds fly north in springtime?

It's way too far to walk!

Where do cows go on their day off?
The Mooseum!

Why was the computer sneezing all day?
It had a really bad virus!

Why couldn't the cross eyed teacher get a job?
She couldn't control her pupils!

What do you call a hippo with a messy room?

A Hippopota Mess!

Where do hamsters go for their vacation?

Hamsterdam!

If a cow and a duck got married, what would you have?

Milk and quackers!

What's another name for two banana peels?
Slippers!

Why did the belt go to jail for 3 years?
He was caught holding up a pair of pants!

Why was the computer feeling so cold?
It's Windows were left open!

Why did the lamb go to the mall?
To go to the baaaaarber shop!

If a plumber married a ballerina, what would their child do?
Become a tap dancer!

What do you call an elephant that didn't have a bath for a year?
A smellyphant!

Funny Knock Knock Jokes!

Knock knock.

Who's there?

Pasta.

Pasta who?

Pasta salt and pepper please!

Knock knock.

Who's there?

Panther.

Panther who?

My Panther falling down! Help!

Knock knock.

Who's there?

Troy.

Troy who?

Troy to be quicker next time please!

Knock knock.

Who's there?

Tick.

Tick who?

Tick 'em up! I'm a wobber!

Knock knock.

Who's there?

Gladys.

Gladys who?

Gladys Friday – I love the weekend!

Yayy!

Knock knock.

Who's there?

Dishes.

Dishes who?

Dishes me, remember?

We met last week!

Knock knock.

Who's there?

Mandy.

Mandy who?

Mandy lifeboats! We're sinking!

Knock knock.

Who's there?

Ivor.

Ivor who?

Ivor cold hands from waiting so long!

Knock knock.

Who's there?

Sienna.

Sienna who?

Sienna good movies lately?

Knock knock.

Who's there?

Abel.

Abel who?

Abel would mean I don't have to knock!

Knock knock.

Who's there?

House.

House who?

House about letting me in before I fall asleep!

Knock knock.

Who's there?

Robin.

Robin who?

Robin you! Hands up and fill my bag with money!

Knock knock.

Who's there?

Alby.

Alby who?

Alby back in a minute, so just wait there please!

Knock knock.

Who's there?

Irish.

Irish who?

Irish I was taller. Then I could reach the doorbell!

Knock knock.

Who's there?

Ice cream.

Ice cream who?

Ice Cream if you don't open this door

right now!

Knock knock.

Who's there?

Weirdo.

Weirdo who?

Weirdo you want me to put your

parcel, sir? Please sign here.

Knock knock.

Who's there?

Carmen.

Carmen who?

Carmen get your hotdogs!

Fresh hotdogs for sale!

Knock knock.

Who's there?

Wilfred.

Wilfred who?

Wilfred be able to come out to play?

Knock knock.

Who's there?

Adair.

Adair who?

Adair when I was younger but now I'm bald!

Knock knock.

Who's there?

Adam.

Adam who?

If you Adam up I'll pay half the bill!

Knock knock.

Who's there?

Delta.

Delta who?

Delta great hand in a card game last night!

Knock knock.

Who's there?

Saul.

Saul who?

Saul there is - there isn't any more!

Knock knock.

Who's there?

Yah.

Yah who?

Yah who! Ride 'em cowboy!

Knock knock.

Who's there?

Courtney.

Courtney who?

Courtney good movies lately?

Knock knock.

Who's there?

Miniature.

Miniature who?

Miniature let me in I'll pay you that money I owe you!

Knock knock.

Who's there?

Mariel.

Mariel who?

Mariel name is top secret!

Knock knock.

Who's there?

Wilma.

Wilma who?

Wilma key ever work on this door?

Knock knock.

Who's there?

Justin.

Justin who?

Justin case I forget my key can you leave it out for me?

Knock knock.

Who's there?

Owl.

Owl who?

Owl be sure to use the doorbell tomorrow!

Knock knock.

Who's there?

Herd.

Herd who?

I herd you were home. Why didn't you call?

Knock knock.

Who's there?

Claire.

Claire who?

Claire the way! I need to use the bathroom! Quickly!

Knock knock.

Who's there?

Toby.

Toby who?

Toby or not to be, that is the question!

Knock knock.

Who's there?

Maul.

Maul who?

Let's go to the Maul and buy some treats!

Knock knock.

Who's there?

Betty.

Betty who?

Betty you can't guess how many times I have knocked on this door!

Knock knock.

Who's there?

Norway.

Norway who?

That's Norway to talk to a friend!

Knock knock.

Who's there?

Sarah.

Sarah who?

Is Sarah another way we can open this door?

Knock knock.

Who's there?

Heaven.

Heaven who?

I'm Heaven a party on Friday. Want to come?

Knock knock.

Who's there?

Cain.

Cain who?

Cain you give me a lift to school? I'm really late!!

Knock knock.

Who's there?

Elsa.

Elsa who?

Who Elsa do you think it would be?

Let me in!

Knock knock.

Who's there?

Harry.

Harry who?

Harry up! Let's go!

Knock knock.

Who's there?

Diesel.

Diesel who?

Diesel be the best holidays ever!

Knock knock.

Who's there?

Poor me.

Poor me who?

Poor me a glass of water! I'm really thirsty!

Knock knock.

Who's there?

Esther.

Esther who?

Esther any way this door can open faster?

Knock knock.

Who's there?

Onya.

Onya who?

Onya marks! Go!

Knock knock.

Who's there?

Ivan.

Ivan who?

Ivan appointment to see you today!

Knock knock.

Who's there?

Ben.

Ben who?

Ben knocking so long I forgot why

I'm here!

Knock knock.

Who's there?

Goliath.

Goliath who?

Goliath down if you're a bit sleepy!

Knock knock.

Who's there?

Wendy.

Wendy who?

Wendy doorbell works, please let me know!

Knock knock.

Who's there?

Maya.

Maya who?

Maya come in? It's an emergency!

Knock knock.

Who's there?

Quack.

Quack who?

These jokes totally quack me up!

Let's read some more!

Knock knock.

Who's there?

Egg.

Egg who?

It's so Eggciting to see you again!

Knock knock.

Who's there?

Doughnut.

Doughnut who?

I Doughnut know but I will find out!

Knock knock.

Who's there?

Candice.

Candice who?

Candice bell actually ring because I have pressed it 12 times already!

Knock knock.

Who's there?

Mary.

Mary who?

Mary Christmas to you and a happy new year!

Knock knock.

Who's there?

Bed.

Bed who?

Bed you I can run faster than you.

Ready, set, GO!!

Knock knock.

Who's there?

Irish.

Irish who?

Irish the rain would stop!

Knock knock.

Who's there?

Kermit.

Kermit who?

Kermit any crimes and the police will get you!

Knock knock.

Who's there?

UCI.

UCI who?

UCI am going to the park. Want to come?

Knock knock.

Who's there?

Toucan.

Toucan who?

Toucan play at this game you know!

Knock knock.

Who's there?

Ray.

Ray who?

Ray member when we first met?

Love at first sight!

Funny Riddles!

What can you catch but never throw?
A cold!

What goes up but never comes down?
Your age!

Why is an island like the letter T?
It's in the middle of water!

What can clap but has no hands?
Thunder!

What gets whiter the dirtier it gets?
A chalkboard!

People buy me to eat and never eat me.
What am I?
A fork!

Which lion is the best swimmer?
The sea lion!

What starts with a P, ends with an E, but has hundreds of letters?
Post Office!

What has 4 legs but never runs?
A table!

What is the most curious letter?

Y!

What can you break without even touching it?

A promise!

What never asks questions but is always answered?

A doorbell!

Which word becomes shorter if you add 2 letters to it?

Short!

What starts with "e" and ends with "e" but contains one letter?

Envelope!

Which kind of room has no doors or windows?

A mushroom!

The more you take, the more you leave behind. What am I?

Footsteps!

Which letter of the alphabet has the most water?

C!

How can a pocket be empty but still have something in it?

It has a hole in it!

Why is the letter A like a flower?
The B is after it!

What always sleeps with its shoes on?
A horse!

What has feathers but no wings?
A pillow!

Feed me and I grow. Give me a drink and I die. What am I?

Fire!

What has many rings but no fingers?

A telephone!

Which word is always spelt wrong?

Wrong!

I'm tall when I'm young but short when I'm old. What am I?

A candle!

What has a neck but no head?

A bottle!

Which side of a chicken has the most feathers?

The outside!

Which word contains 26 letters but only 3 syllables?

Alphabet!

What begins with T, ends with T and has T in it?

Teapot!

You can see me in water but I am never wet. What am I?

Your reflection!

What has hands but cannot clap?
A clock!

What comes down but never goes up?
Rain!

How much dirt is in a 3 feet deep hole?
None. It's a hole!

Which word can be written forwards or backwards but still read the same?

NOON!

What was the highest mountain before Mount Everest was discovered?

Mount Everest. It was still there but hadn't been discovered yet!

What has 4 eyes but cannot see?

Mississippi!

Funny Tongue Twisters!

Tongue Twisters are great fun!
Start off slow.
How fast can you go?

Swiss wrist watches.
Swiss wrist watches.
Swiss wrist watches.

Watching washing wash.
Watching washing wash.
Watching washing wash.

Clumsy clowns crushed king clown's crowns.
Clumsy clowns crushed king clown's crowns.
Clumsy clowns crushed king clown's crowns.

Freshly fried flying fish.
Freshly fried flying fish.
Freshly fried flying fish.

She sees seas slapping shores.
She sees seas slapping shores.
She sees seas slapping shores.

Scissors sizzle, thistles sizzle.
Scissors sizzle, thistles sizzle.
Scissors sizzle, thistles sizzle.

How much wood would a woodchuck chuck
if a woodchuck could chuck wood?
How much wood would a woodchuck chuck
if a woodchuck could chuck wood?
How much wood would a woodchuck chuck
if a woodchuck could chuck wood?

Fred threw fast throws.
Fred threw fast throws.
Fred threw fast throws.

Bad money mad bunny.
Bad money mad bunny.
Bad money mad bunny.

Tie twine to three tree twigs.
Tie twine to three tree twigs.
Tie twine to three tree twigs.

Three fleas flew through.
Three fleas flew through.
Three fleas flew through.

Sammy likes slimy slugs.
Sammy likes slimy slugs.
Sammy likes slimy slugs.

Six slowly sliding slippery snails.
Six slowly sliding slippery snails.
Six slowly sliding slippery snails.

Black background, brown background.
Black background, brown background.
Black background, brown background.

Silly sheep weep and sleep.
Silly sheep weep and sleep.
Silly sheep weep and sleep.

Which witch wished which wicked wish?
Which witch wished which wicked wish?
Which witch wished which wicked wish?

I wish to wash my Irish wristwatch.
I wish to wash my Irish wristwatch.
I wish to wash my Irish wristwatch.

The queen in green screams.
The queen in green screams.
The queen in green screams.

Four furious friends fly forward.
Four furious friends fly forward.
Four furious friends fly forward.

Geese gobble grass.
Geese gobble grass.
Geese gobble grass.

The gum glue grew glum.
The gum glue grew glum.
The gum glue grew glum.

Billy builds big blocks.
Billy builds big blocks.
Billy builds big blocks.

A proper copper coffee pot.
A proper copper coffee pot.
A proper copper coffee pot.

Bonus Funny Jokes!

What did the doctor say to the patient who thought he was an alligator?

Snap out of it!

Where did the alien get a coffee?

Starbucks!

Why did the pony stop singing in the farm band?

She was a little hoarse!

Why did the cow eat all your grass?
It was a lawn moo-er!

Why did the tiger spit out the clown?
He tasted funny!

What kind of tie does a boy pig wear?
A pigsty!

How do divers sleep under the sea?

They use a snore-kel!

What did the doctor say to the patient who thought he was an elevator?

Lucky you can stop at this floor!

What time is it when an elephant sits on your lunch box?

Time to get a new lunch box!

What is the quietest dog in the world?
A hush puppy!

Why did the orange fall asleep at work?
He ran out of juice!

What is the proper name for a dinosaur in high heels?
MyFeetAreReallySaurus!

What game do tornadoes play at parties?
Twister!

What do acrobats do on hot days?
Summer saults!

What was written on the robot's gravestone?
Rust in Peace!

What do snakes do after an argument?
Hiss and make up!

What is Santa's cat called?
Santa Claws!

What did the doctor say to the patient who had a weird ringing in his ear?
Have you tried answering it?

What did the cow say on January the 1st?
Happy Moo Year!

Which animal is very flexible?
Yoga bear!

Why did the cat jump up on the computer?
So she could catch the mouse!

What happens if it's been raining cats and dogs?

You might step in a poodle!

Why did the boy take 3 rolls of toilet paper to the birthday party?

He was a party pooper!

Why did the butterfly leave the dance?

It was a moth ball!

What do you call a lion that likes to wear top hats?

A dandy lion!

What do you call an elephant that didn't have a bath for a year?

A smellyphant!

What was the pirate's favorite subject at school?

Arrrrrt!

Why was the lamp sad at the beach?
He forgot to bring his shades!

Why did the teacher wear dark sunglasses?
Her students were too bright!

How do monsters keep their hair so neat?
With scare spray!

Why are porcupines so likeable?
They have allot of good points!

What do you call a boy with a calculator in his pocket?
Smarty Pants!

Where did the baby fruit have a sleep?
In an apri-cot!

Why did the clock have a holiday?
He needed to unwind!

What shoes do chickens wear to the gym?
Re bok bok boks!

Why are pirates pirates?
Because they ARRRRRRRRRR!!

Bonus

Knock Knock Jokes!

Knock knock.

Who's there?

Dish.

Dish who?

Dish is a very nice house you have!

Knock knock.

Who's there?

Viper.

Viper who?

Viper nose before you get sick!

Knock knock.

Who's there?

Gorilla.

Gorilla who?

I can gorilla burger for you for your lunch if you like!

Knock knock.

Who's there?

Tank.

Tank who?

Tank goodness you finally answered the door!

Knock knock.

Who's there?

Amanda.

Amanda who?

Amanda repair that window you broke wants to charge me $300!

Knock knock.

Who's there?

Howard.

Howard who?

Howard you like to knock for a change?

Knock knock.

Who's there?

Jupiter.

Jupiter who?

Jupiter invite in my letterbox? It looks like your writing!

Knock knock.

Who's there?

Tunis.

Tunis who?

Tunis company but three's a crowd!

Knock knock.

Who's there?

Alex.

Alex who?

Alex plain it all to you in a minute!

Let me in!

Knock knock.

Who's there?

Norma Lee.

Norma Lee who?

Norma Lee I wouldn't knock but I forgot my key!

Knock knock.

Who's there?

Keanu

Keanu who?

Keanu open this door before I freeze to death!

Knock knock.

Who's there?

Honeydew.

Honeydew who?

Honeydew you want to hear lots more jokes?

Knock knock.

Who's there?

Gino.

Gino who?

Gino me really well so open the door!

Knock knock.

Who's there?

Wok.

Wok who?

Wok and woll baby!

Knock knock.

Who's there?

Gwen.

Gwen who?

Gwen you have finished your homework, let's go fishing!

Knock knock.

Who's there?

Poll.

Poll who?

Poll iceman John here. You're under arrest!

Knock knock.

Who's there?

Area.

Area who?

Area deaf! I've been knocking for 2 days!

Knock knock.

Who's there?

Barbie.

Barbie who?

Barbie Q for dinner! Yummy!

Knock knock.

Who's there?

Boo.

Boo who?

Don't cry so much, it's only a joke!

Knock knock.

Who's there?

Pop.

Pop who?

Pop on over to my place. We're having ice cream!

Knock knock.

Who's there?

Frank.

Frank who?

Frank you very much for finally opening this door!

Knock knock.

Who's there?

Chicken.

Chicken who?

Let's chicken to that new hotel in town!

Knock knock.

Who's there?

Icing.

Icing who?

Icing so loud I need earplugs!

Knock knock.

Who's there?

Pasta.

Pasta who?

It's Pasta your bedtime! Quick!

Into bed!

Thank you so much

For reading our book.

I hope you have enjoyed these funny jokes for 8 year old kids as much as my kids and I did as we were putting this book together.

We really had a lot of fun and laughter creating and compiling this book and we really appreciate you for reading our book.

If you could possibly let us know what you thought of our book by way of a review we would really appreciate it 😊

To see all our latest books or leave a review just go to
kidsjokebooks.com
Once again, thanks so much for reading.

All the best,
Jimmy Jones
And also Ella & Alex (the kids)
And even Obi (the dog – he's very cute!)
